This Ladybird Book belongs to:

_____

_____

_____

_____

All children
have a great ambition …
to read by themselves.

Through traditional and popular stories, each title
in the **Read It Yourself** series introduces children to
the most commonly used words in the English
language (*Key Words*), plus additional words
necessary to tell the story.
The additional words appearing in this book are
listed below.

shoemaker, wife, leather,
cuts, shoes, morning,
sells, hide, elves, clothes, happy

Ladybird books are widely available, but in case of
difficulty may be ordered by post or telephone from:

Ladybird Books – Cash Sales Department
Littlegate Road Paignton Devon TQ3 3BE
Telephone 0803 554761

A catalogue record for this book is available
from the British Library

Published by Ladybird Books Ltd Loughborough Leicestershire UK
Ladybird Books Inc Auburn Maine 04210 USA

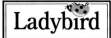

The Elves
and the
Shoemaker

by Fran Hunia
illustrated by John Dyke

The shoemaker
and his wife
have no money.

The shoemaker
is in his shop.

He has
some leather.

He cuts out
some shoes.

The shoemaker says,
I want to go
to bed.
I can make the shoes
in the morning.

In the morning
the shoemaker
sees some shoes
in his shop.

Did *you* make
the shoes?
he says.

No, says his wife.

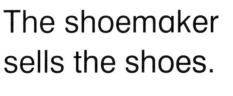

The shoemaker
sells the shoes.

He has some money
for more leather.

I can make
some more shoes,
he says.

The shoemaker
cuts out
some more shoes.

He and his wife
go to bed.

In the morning
the shoemaker
comes into his shop
to make the shoes.

Look,
says the shoemaker.

Did *you*
make the shoes?

No, says his wife.

The shoemaker sells the shoes.

He has some money for more leather.

The shoemaker says,
I want to see
who makes the shoes
for us.

We can hide
and see who comes.

The shoemaker
cuts out
some shoes.

He and his wife hide.

They look to see
who comes.

Some elves come
into the shop.

The elves work
and the shoemaker
and his wife look.

The elves
make the shoes.

The elves
go home.

The shoemaker
and his wife
come out
to see the shoes.

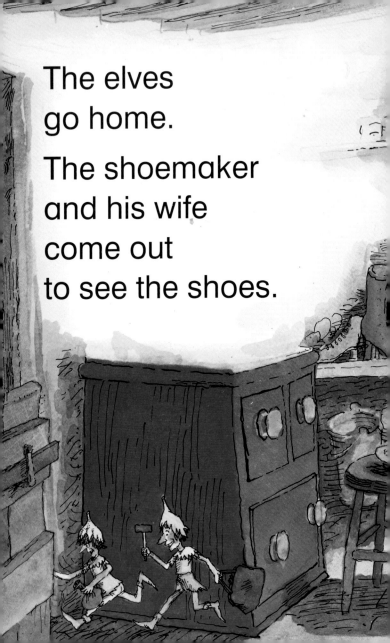

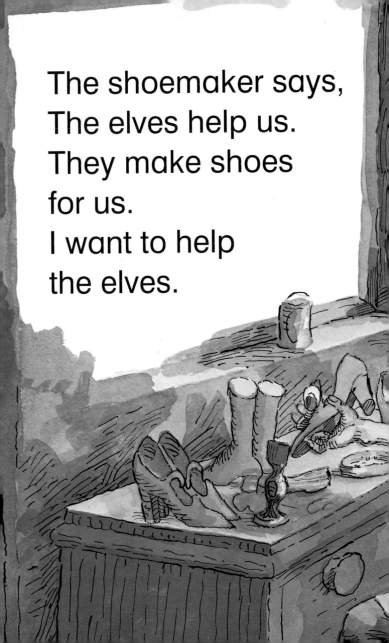

The shoemaker says,
The elves help us.
They make shoes
for us.
I want to help
the elves.

They make
some clothes
and shoes for the elves.

They work
and work.

Here are
the clothes
and the shoes.

The shoemaker
and his wife
go and hide.

The elves come into the shop.

Look, they say. Here are some clothes for us.

The elves like
the clothes.

They have fun in
the shop.

The elves go home.

They are happy.

The shoemaker
and his wife
have a lot of money
and they are happy.

LADYBIRD
READING SCHEMES

Read It Yourself links with all Ladybird reading schemes and can be used with any other method of learning to read.

Say the Sounds

Ladybird's **Say the Sounds** graded reading scheme is a *phonics* scheme. It teaches children the sounds of individual letters and letter combinations, enabling them to tackle new words by building them up as a blend of smaller units.

There are 8 titles in this scheme:

1 Rocket to the jungle
2 Frog and the lollipops
3 The go-cart race
4 Pirate's treasure
5 Humpty Dumpty and the robots
6 Flying saucer
7 Dinosaur rescue
8 The accident

Support material available: Practice Books, Double Cassette pack, Flash Cards